MW00977311

A TOY'S JOURNEY

A Tale of Lost and Found Treasure

Written & Illustrated by

Madeleine J. Kurtz

Copyright © 2014 Madeleine J. Kurtz

All rights reserved.

All rights reserved to include trademark on all graphics.
No part of this book may be reproduced, stored in a
retrieval system, or transmitted by any means, electronic,
mechanical, photocopying, recording, or otherwise,
without written permission from the author.

ISBN-13: 978-0-692-30951-3

Book & cover design by Darlene Swanson
of Van-garde Imagery, Inc.

DEDICATION

This book is dedicated to my parents, John and Jean Kurtz.
Thank you for always encouraging me and supporting
me in my writing. You guys are awesome! I also want to
thank God and His wonderful leadership in my life.
Without Him, I would be nothing.

CONTENTS

Acknowledgments vii

1   Bonnie 1

2   Joey Capanilla 3

3   Don Capanilla 7

4   Sally Hatfield – A Tribute 11

5   Saranaa Lung 15

6   The Monkey, The Man, The Boy called
Peter, and Mina his Cousin 17

7   The Rest of the Story 19

ACKNOWLEDGMENTS

I'd like to first thank God for giving me the gift of writing and my parents for all of their loving support. And of course, Mrs. Bonnie Hennessy whose story of the toy Santa my book was based on and whose permission I have to retell it in my own way. And Darlene Swanson for her formatting skills.

BONNIE

It was a year Bonnie could never forget. She was thirteen years old and her parents had gotten divorced. It was nearing Christmas time, and Bonnie was yearning to open the boxes of Christmas decorations, especially the box containing the ten inch rubber Santa Claus she held dear.

As long as she could remember her Christmases had been accompanied by the silly little Saint Nick with the black-mittened hand waving a happy "hello"; it reminded her of her intact family and the constancy of it all.

Time to open the boxes! She reached for the box with Santa in it but... HE WAS GONE!!!!

Bonnie franticly searched the boxes but in vain. She ran to her mother and cried "where has Santa gone?!" Her mother wearily sighed, "I got rid of him! I'm sorry, dear I didn't know you still wanted it"

Bonnie ran next door to her best friend's house and threw herself into her friend's mother's arms and sobbed "Mama accidentally threw away Santa!" At that moment, the distraught girl looked up and saw the garbage truck having just picked up its load, pulling away from the curb with Santa tied on the grill of the truck—a garbage man's attempt at holiday cheer! "And there he goes!" she cried.

That was the last Bonnie saw of her little Santa, and with her that day, something else seemed to go away...

...something in her heart.

JOEY CAPONILLA

At that same time 18 year old Joey Caponilla had just finished tying the decoration he'd picked out of a torn garbage bag onto the garbage truck he was driving. He was a ruddy, dark-haired, Italian boy whose father, grandfather, and great-grandfather had all been garbage men. Now he was a garbage man too. The hours were long and the pay was little but it was okay, for now. His secret dream was to marry his childhood sweetheart, Gracie Yewdon, and to own a deli in Cape May, New Jersey overlooking the ocean.

Why, might you ask, would he want to own a deli? Let me tell you a story. When Joey was growing up, he was very alone. He never knew his mother. His only brother was twenty three and in prison. His twin sister, Lea, was very sickly and had to constantly stay in bed. His father, he never saw, because he would leave for work at the crack of dawn and get home at midnight.

Joey's only friend was Mrs. Xela Wilnigroski, the Polish wife of the deli owner across the street. Because his family was poor, Joey had gone many a night hungry.

But Mrs. Xela took pity on him and when he came into the deli to buy a small sandwich for him and Lea to share, she would take the bread from the middle of the loaf so that it was bigger and more meat could fit in one sandwich. Even more, she would give him an 80% discount and send him off with two fresh, hot cookies. To Joey, that deli reminded him of kindness and family. That's why he wanted to own one of his own.

Now back to the real story!

After the holidays, the garbage men decided to throw away the rubber Santa. But suddenly Joey felt a connection with the Santa.

He felt they both had wasted talents and they both had a better purpose. So Joey, when no one was looking, quickly hid the Santa under his coat. In the end, Joey did own a deli in Cape May, New Jersey, he married Gracie Yewdon on the beach, and they had 8 kids.

What happened to Santa you ask? Well let's find out!

DON CAPONILLA

One fateful day a man walked into the deli. He was Don Caponilla, Joey's brother who had been in jail for many years. Mean old Don wanted money and he and Joey had a big fight. Joey had the last say, and a frustrated, and vengeful Don stormed out of the Deli. Before he left, he grabbed the only thing that he could think of to hurt his little brother--the Santa Claus on the shelf behind the cash register.

For many months, Don Caponilla wondered aimlessly, hitchhiking from town to town up and down the eastern seaboard. A few times he tried to sell or trade the Santa Claus, (because it made him think of his brother which made him feel guilty) but somehow he couldn't bring himself to get rid of his brother's old good luck charm.

So in the end he threw it into the river, a symbol of all the frustration he had in his life. As he watched St. Nick disappear into the cold black water, Don Caponilla made a decision that changed his life forever… he jumped in after Santa, intending to end it all.

But his life didn't end that night. Moments after Don's plunge into the icy water, a passing yacht fished the despairing Italian derelict out of the drink, now unconscious while the rubber talisman (Santa) bobbed off into the night.

Don's life changed that fateful night, and when he awoke from his unconsciousness, he vowed that he would make good with his life, now suddenly precious to him. Don Caponilla became a pianist and part time masseur.

SALLY HATFIELD – A TRIBUTE

As Santa bobbled into the morning mist, a young girl named Sally Hatfield was by the riverbank picking flowers. She saw a little rubber thing in the water. "Nasty rubbish I suppose. Why do people have to litter!", she muttered to herself. She took off her shoes and waded in the water to retrieve the "rubbish" to throw it away properly.

Sally soon realized it wasn't trash at all, it was a sweet little Santa Claus figure. So Sally picked it up and took it home. Oh she loved it! She would sleep with it and she would play with it.

When Sally turned twelve, a great disaster fell upon the Hatfield family. Sally got extremely ill and it looked like she wasn't going to get better. Everyone had lost hope that she would recover and her parents feared the worst.

One terrible day, Sally called her mother in. "Mama" she said weakly, "I need to go home to Jesus….*cough*" Her mother wept in anguish. "Mama…*cough*…could you please give my ruby ring to Sarah and my Santa to Saranaa my pen pal in Thailand." Sally went into a fit of coughing then uttered what many thought would be her last words. "I love you Mama…*cough* I love you…."

She fell unconscious. Her distraught mother quickly put Santa in a box to be sent to Thailand and returned to her dying daughter's side. But miraculously, a doctor burst into the hospital room and announced that he had found the cure to Sally's illness. Sally made a full recovery and Santa's journey continued.

SARANAA LUNG

Santa was long gone by the time Sally recovered. Santa flew by air to China, then by boat to Japan, finally flying to Thailand into a young Thai girl's arms. Her name was Saranaa Lung. She was mother-less, father-less, sister-less, brother-less, uncle-less, aunt-less, grandpa-less, grandma-less, and cousin-less. She was an orphan with no past, and most likely no future either. As the woman who ran the five orphan-ages handed her the parcel she muttered, "who would give this little brat something?"

Saranaa opened the package. All it said was from Sally to Saranaa. There was a small rubber thing in the box, and the smart Saranaa knew it was called a Father Christmas.

On that day, her life changed forever. The prince himself came to the orphanage. He wanted to adopt a little girl because he and his beloved wife could not have children of their own. Now the girls all lined up and the prince chose, guess who?

Saranaa went off to live in a golden palace with lots of servants and maids and pretty dresses. But Santa's trek would continue.

THE MONKEY, THE MAN, THE BOY CALLED PETER, AND MINA HIS COUSIN

A meddlesome monkey sneaked into Saranaa's bedroom at night and stole jewels, gems, broaches, and the rubber Father Christmas. The monkey then went off to its lair in the ruined temple.

The monkey had lots of jewels. One night a treasure hunter came and shooed off the monkey. He greedily gathered up all the gems but the Santa Claus also caught his eye. He picked it up and sent it to his favorite nephew, Peter, in Russia. Peter in turn, sent it to his cousin Mina, who lived in Kentucky. Mina sold Santa in a flea market to a lady from Tennessee....

She put him in her antique store. So after a 40 year journey the toy ended up in Franklin, Tennessee, just another item on display.   But who walked into that very antique shop? The now grown up girl Bonnie! It was a miracle that the two found each other 40 years later and that makes this truly a tale of lost and found treasure.

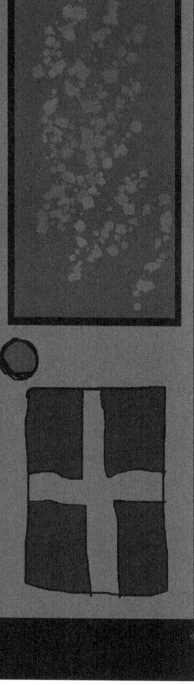

THE REST OF THE STORY

This story is true, at least in part. Bonnie really did live in a house in New Jersey and really did love a little rubber Santa. The last she saw of Santa was when he was tied to the grill of a garbage truck being driven away into the December cold of 1970.

Life went on. Bonnie grew up, got married, had children of her own, and hardly thought of the little Santa she had lost as a child. She left New Jersey and settled in Tennessee.

It was late fall in the year 2007 when the strings of fate tugged Bonnie back to her childhood. She was walking through the antique shops of Franklin, Tennessee when her eye was caught by a bizarrely familiar sight that immediately took her back to her past. It was her vintage Santa, and as fantastic as it sounds, it was the same one she had lost nearly forty years before. In his foot was a broken squeaker; the same one Bonnie had remembered breaking when she was six. Across his rubber waist was the mark of a belt where he had been strapped to the grill of a garbage truck. She recognized him immediately and with the recollection came all the memories and pain that had swirled around the time he was lost.

But Bonnie didn't buy the Santa from the antique store that day. No, the price of $30 for a silly antique toy was not the sort of thing her practical mind could justify, so she left it in the display window.

Over a coffee with friends, Bonnie mentioned the strangeness of seeing an object from her youth so magically transported across state lines and into the very store she had visited. It was like fate, she thought, that such a crazy thing could happen. My mother, Bonnie's good friend, asked her why she hadn't pounced on buying the Santa if its very existence in the store was so unfathomably incredible.

Bonnie shrugged, money doesn't grow on trees and the economy isn't good. My mother, however, refused to accept that such a fantastic thing would be allowed to be lost again. My mother asked Bonnie to text a picture she had taken of it, so she could tell the story to me, her daughter.

So my mother and I went to the store and bought the Santa. I was ten at the time, a quiet girl with a head full of stories and a nose perpetually in a book. I was fascinated by the idea of an object traveling so far in time and space. I held it in my hands as my mother began to wrap it as a Christmas present for Bonnie.

"I wonder where this little guy has been?" I asked as I studied his little round face and the indentation where a belt buckle had cut into his fat belly.

"Who knows?" My mom said as she placed him in a gift box. "It was over forty years. He could have travelled around the world for all we know."

I looked at the little Santa and I wondered. *Where did you go?*

My mom suddenly looked up, her eyes bright with a sudden idea. "What if you write a story about what Santa's been doing all these last few years?"

"I don't know..." I said worriedly, "I've never really written any-thing before."

"You have such a big imagination Maddie! I'm sure you'd write a good story!" My mom said reassuringly.

So I started writing. Christmas drew nearer and the world of the Santa Claus doll started to take shape. I thought of all the places he could have gone to, all the characters he could have met. As I furiously typed out the story on my tubular Dell from the prehistoric caveman times of 1998, I felt myself relishing in the act of creating the sentences in my story. As each chapter took shape on the screen, I felt more and more confident and daring.

I wrapped up the story just in time for our family to join Bonnie's family in the iconic Christmas tradition of constructing miniature sugar domiciles you may call Gingerbread Houses.

My mother and I had been plotting for the perfect moment to surprise Bonnie with the Santa and his newly written story, and there was no better time to unleash our gift than on Gingerbread Day. We carefully sealed up the Santa in his gift box and rolled the story into a little silver tube like a scroll.

We arrived at Bonnie's house that night, my mother and me both shaking in nervous anticipation. We walked into the kitchen where Bonnie was just finishing up the baking of little gingerbread walls and roofs for the little cookie people to live inside of. We sat down at the table covered in dozens of bowls of miscellaneous candies and icing and I felt my heart beating out of my chest in anxiousness as my father nodded at my mother to bring out the story I had written.

"Bonnie," My mom began, her voice strong and warm, without the tinge of nerves I had, "You know that Santa you found in that antique store? Well, I told Maddie about it and she wrote a story about where the Santa went during those 40 years. Would you like me to read it?"

Bonnie set the tray of gingerbread down to cool and sat down in the chair across from us, a curious smile on her face. Her family gathered around ours as my mom began the story, this story. I listened as my mother read it and found myself laughing at the melodramatic parts and cringing at places where I may have gone a bit too sensational.

The whole time I watched Bonnie's face as she listened to it, and as we neared the end, I saw the emotion begin to well up in her eyes. As the final chapter ended with the Santa in the thrift store, my father snuck out behind Bonnie and brought in the Santa itself, wrapped up in a gift box.

"Now the rest of the Santa story is for you to finish." My mother said softly. Tears came streaming down Bonnie's face as she opened up the box and saw her old childhood toy in front of her.

Looking back on that night, I don't think it was the Santa itself that made the moment so beautiful, even though it was miraculous that she found him again after four decades of his absence. I don't think it was the gift on its own, but the love behind the gift.

My mother and I wanted to do something special for someone else, and I think that idea of love transcending time and space is parallel to the journey of Santa. We wanted Bonnie to know that we would always love her regardless of the years and the physical distance that would come between us. Even though my Santa Story is just a silly little story written by a silly little girl, the love that was shared on that night with the gingerbread is something that makes even the most ridiculous and far-fetched of tales seem important and meaningful.

To this day when Christmas comes near, Bonnie's family and my family read the Santa Story I wrote, and even though getting older has made me cover my eyes in embarrassment at some of my more hammy passages, I still appreciate how the story has brought us all together.

I hope you have enjoyed my Santa Story. God bless.

Madeleine Kurtz – October 2014

The real Bonnie with the real Santa

PHOTO COURTESY: MISTY WESTEBBE - NEWDAYPHOTOGRAPHY.NET

PHOTO COURTESY: MISTY WESTEBBE - NEWDAYPHOTOGRAPHY.NET

ABOUT THE AUTHOR

Maddie Kurtz was 10 years old and a Williamson County School student attending Scales Elementary School in Brentwood, Tennessee when she wrote this story. She also illustrated the story in 2014. Maddie plans to attend college and major in English and Business and whatever God leads. She loves God, writing, history, art, and cats. Especially cats!

www.MaddieKurtz.com

CPSIA information can be obtained at www.ICGtesting.com
Printed in the USA
BVOW10*2143011214

377519BV00004B/17/P